# Monkeys Wearing Tennis Shoes

## by Rachel Bridwell

Illustrated by Steve Weaver

the PeppertreePress LLC
Sarasota, Florida

For information regarding permission,
call 941-922-2662 or contact us at our website:
www.peppertreepublishing.com or write to:
the Peppertree Press, LLC.
Attention: Publisher
1269 First Street, Suite 7
Sarasota, Florida 34236

ISBN: 978-1-61493-736-4

Library of Congress Number: 2020917220

Printed October 2020

I dedicate this book to my three
monkeys, Adalyn, Liam and Chandler.

Monkey see,
monkey do,
monkeys wearing
tennis shoes!

4

Monkeys don't wear
tennis shoes!
Yes, they do!
Yes, they do!

One is red,
and one is blue!

# What do monkeys do
# when they wear tennis shoes?

They run,

and jump,

and yell, "EEE EWE EWE!"

Those silly monkeys!
Jumping up and down!

# Now they are running all over town!

They run down the street and
into a store, knocking down food
all over the floor!

The monkeys giggle as they run.
Grabbing bananas, oh what fun!

The Butcher, the Baker,
the Candlestick Maker
all gasp at the sight.

# What a sight to see!

# Little monkeys running
# so fast down the street!

They run so fast
and they jump so high.
Look at that,
they can touch the sky!

16

Those silly monkeys
better slow down.
If they run too fast
they could fall on the ground.

17

Have you ever seen a monkey
with a boo-boo? Not me!
But I think they would cry and say,
"Wee Wee Wee!"

Those monkeys look tired
from all that running around.
They take off their shoes
and they sit right down.

19

Those monkeys look
hungry and thirsty.

Let's get them
something to eat.

A tasty banana and some juice
sounds like a good treat.
They eat their bananas
and they drink some juice.

And think to themselves,
what fun that was wearing
tennis shoes!

CPSIA information can be obtained
at www.ICGtesting.com
Printed in the USA
LVHW071956250621
691198LV00001B/18